How to use this book

Follow the advice, in italics, given for teachers on each page.
Praise *the children at every step!*

Detailed guidance is provided in the Read Write Inc. Phonics Handbook

8 reading activities

Children:
* *Practise reading the speed sounds.*
* *Read the green and red words for the story.*
* *Listen as you read the introduction.*
* *Discuss the vocabulary check with you.*
* *Read the story.*
* *Re-read the story and discuss the 'questions to talk about'.*
* *Re-read the story with fluency and expression.*
* *Practise reading the speed words.*

Speed sounds

Consonants *Say the pure sounds (do not add 'uh').*

f ff	l (ll)	m	n	r	s	v ve	z (zz) s	(sh)	(th)	ng (nk)

b (bb)	c k ck	d	g (gg)	h	j	p	qu	t	w wh	x	y	(ch) tch

Vowels *Say the sounds in and out of order.*

at	hen	in	on	up	day	see	high	blow	zoo

*Each box contains one sound but sometimes more than one grapheme. Focus graphemes are **circled**.*

Green words

Read in Fred Talk (sounds).

sme<u>ll</u>   can   nuts   e<u>gg</u>   red   jam   <u>th</u>en   on   hot

fi<u>sh</u>   cut   up   bit   <u>th</u>an<u>k</u>   yum   put

Read the root word first and then with the ending.

<u>ch</u>ip   →   <u>ch</u>ips   rub   →   ru<u>bb</u>ed

Red words

I   s<u>ai</u>d   <u>th</u>e   he   no   <u>you</u>

Vocabulary check

Discuss the meaning (as used in the story) after the children have read the word.

definition:

pizza   *a special Italian bread with lots of toppings*

Punctuation to note in this story:

Zip Pip	*Capital letter for names*
Yum No He	*Capital letters that start sentences*
.	*Full stop at the end of each sentence*
!	*Exclamation mark used to show anger and surprise*
...	*Wait and see*
?	*Question mark*

Pip's pizza

Introduction

Ask:

List all the things that we could put on top of a pizza.

Pip and Zip are aliens. Pip has rolled out some pizza dough and added egg and nuts. Zip is sniffing the air... mmmm! It smells delicious at the moment, but I don't think Pip really knows what else should go on the top of a pizza.

What do you think he might add?

Story written by Gill Munton
Illustrated by Tim Archbold

"Yum, yum!" said Zip.
"I can smell pizza!"

Zip rubbed his tum.

Pip put nuts
on the pizza.

He put an egg
on the pizza.

Then he put red jam
on the pizza!

He put fish
on the pizza!

"Hot pizza!" said Pip.

He cut the pizza up.

"This bit is Zip's," he said.

"No, thank you!" said Zip.

Questions to talk about

FIND IT QUESTIONS

✓ Turn to the page

✓ Read the question to the children

✓ Find the answer

Page 8-9:   Which words tell us that Zip is going to like the pizza?

Page 10:   What did Pip put on the pizza?

Page 11:   What did Pip put on next?

Page 12:   Pip takes the pizza out of the oven. What does he think about the pizza?

Page 13:   Why does Zip say "No, thank you" to Pip? What would you have said?